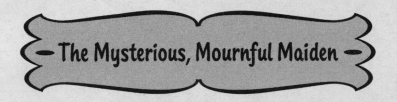

The Mysterious, Mournful Maiden

Princess Power

— The Mysterious, Mournful Maiden —

By Suzanne Williams

Illustrated by Chuck Gonzales

HarperTrophy®
An Imprint of HarperCollinsPublishers

Harper Trophy® is a registered trademark of HarperCollins Publishers.

Library of Congress Cataloging-in-Publication Data
Williams, Suzanne, 1949–
    The mysterious, mournful maiden / by Suzanne Williams ; illustrated by
Chuck Gonzales.— 1st Harper Trophy ed.
        p.   cm. (Princess power ; #4)
    Summary: While the princesses visit eleven-year-old Princess Elena, they
realize the comb that was found must be special when Elena and Lysandra both
dream about a crying young maiden.
    ISBN-10: 0-06-078304-4 (pbk.) — ISBN-13: 978-0-06-078304-4 (pbk.)
    [1. Princesses—Fiction. 2. Friendship—Fiction. 3. Magic—Fiction. 4. Adventure and adventurers—Fiction.] I. Gonzales, Chuck, ill. II. Title.
PZ7.W66824Mys 2007   2006017885
[Fic]—dc22   CIP
                                                                    AC

Typography by Jennifer Heuer
❖
First Harper Trophy edition, 2007

To Sophie Mei Greene,
a very special princess

Contents

Princess Elena

EARLY IN THE EVENING, JUST AS THE SUN WAS setting, Princess Elena went for a walk along the shore. She loved the feel of her bare toes on the warm sand, and the cries of the seagulls made for pleasant company.

A castle by the seaside was a lovely place to live, only sometimes it was also lonely—especially when her father was busy with the affairs of their tiny island. If Elena's mother were still alive, she would have helped to run the kingdom, and King Philip wouldn't have had to work so hard. But, unfortunately, Queen Helen had died eight long years ago, when Elena was only three.

Before long, she passed a group of fishermen reeling in a heavy net. They nodded at her, but whether they recognized her as the king's daughter, she couldn't tell. Shy by nature, she dressed simply so as not to draw attention to herself. Often people were surprised to discover she was King Philip's daughter. She tried not to let that bother her, but sometimes it made her feel invisible.

Glancing toward the horizon, Elena admired the glowing purple sunset. Her friend Princess Fatima had a pair of filmy pantaloons the exact same shade. Fatima was beautiful with her dark skin, long black hair, and almond-shaped eyes. Elena felt mousy by comparison, especially with her frizzy brown hair. No matter how much Elena brushed it, her hair wouldn't lie flat.

If only she had inherited her mother's smooth, silky hair, or had blond waves like her friend Princess Lysandra. That would have been nice too. Sometimes Elena even thought of cutting her hair short, like Princess Tansy, the youngest of her three friends. But cutting her hair would probably only make it bush out all the more. Then she'd wind up looking like a dandelion puff!

Elena wished her friends didn't live so far away. She would love to see them more often. After all, it had been a month since they'd last visited one another at Princess Tansy's castle. Yet sometimes Elena wondered why the other three princesses even included her in their group. They were so much more outgoing and courageous than she.

A flash of brilliant color caught Elena's eye. The sun glinted off an object lying near the water. Elena hurried over to find a comb that was half buried in the sand. She picked it up. No ordinary comb, this one shimmered with all the colors of the rainbow. Elena had never seen anything like it.

Looking closely, she noticed a few long

emerald strands of hair caught in its teeth. What an odd color, she thought. Still, whomever the comb belonged to would surely be sorry to have lost such a beautiful treasure. Slipping the comb into her pocket, Elena turned around, then started back up the beach toward home.

That night, after she'd changed for bed,

Elena carefully washed and dried the gorgeous comb. Unable to resist, she ran it through her frizzy hair. Instead of becoming caught in her tangles, the way other combs did, this one glided effortlessly, like a knife slicing through butter.

Elena ran the comb through her hair several more times, then glanced in the mirror. She was amazed to see that her frizzy locks appeared much softer and looser than usual. They also had a glossy sheen to them, which looked almost golden.

Smiling at her reflection, Elena patted her hair. The girl in the mirror looked . . . well, *pretty*. Elena kissed the comb and laid it carefully on top of her dresser. Then she walked down the hall to say good night to her father.

"Come in," King Philip said when she knocked. Elena pushed open the heavy wooden door and stepped into his room. Her father sat at his desk, official papers spread out before him. Though his eyes looked tired, he managed a smile. "I'm sorry I've been so busy lately," he apologized. "I wanted to eat dinner with you tonight, but I had to settle a dispute between two shop owners, and then . . ."

"It's okay, Father," said Elena, stooping to hug him. "I understand. I only wish there was some way I could help."

King Philip hugged her back. "Let's not think about work right now. Tell me what you've been up to."

Elena described her day. Then she stepped away from her father. "Notice anything different?" she asked, tossing her hair.

Scratching his bald head, King Philip asked, "Is that a new nightgown you're wearing?"

"No," said Elena, glancing down at her peach-colored nightie. Her father had given it to her last Christmas, but that wasn't the kind of detail he'd remember. "It's my *hair*!" she exclaimed. "Doesn't it look different to you?"

"I'm not sure. Did you cut it?"

Elena shook her head no. Then she described the beautiful rainbow-colored comb she'd found on the beach. "I used it tonight," she said. "Don't you think my hair looks smoother than usual? Prettier, maybe?"

"You always look pretty to me," said her father.

Elena smiled. She supposed he'd say that no matter how her hair looked. "Can you have breakfast with me tomorrow?" she asked.

"I can, and I will," he said. "And that's a promise."

"Good," said Elena. Whenever her father made a promise, he kept it, no matter how busy he was. She kissed him good night, then returned to her room.

That night Elena had a very strange

dream. She saw the face of a lovely maiden with flowing emerald hair swimming in a dark, starless sky. "Please," the young woman begged. "Won't you give me back my comb?" The maiden's dark eyes were so full of sorrow, Elena thought her *own* heart would break. She awoke with a start. Just who was this mysterious, mournful maiden?

Lost Item

ELENA LONGED TO KEEP THE BEAUTIFUL COMB for herself. But regardless of whether or not the green-haired maiden existed, she decided she must try to find the comb's rightful owner. After breakfast with her father, she hand lettered a dozen signs and sent a messenger to post them around the kingdom. The signs read:

LOST ITEM FOUND ON BEACH.

SEE PRINCESS ELENA TO IDENTIFY AND CLAIM.

By afternoon there was a long line of people waiting to see her in the Great Hall. A young man was the first to approach. "Good afternoon, Princess," he said boldly. "I've come to claim what you found on the beach."

"You may if it's yours," Elena replied. "Did you lose something there?"

He smiled. "I might have. You didn't find a bag of gold, perhaps? Or a treasure chest filled with jewels?"

Elena shook her head. "I'm afraid not."

"Oh, well," the young man said good-naturedly. "I suppose it was a lot to hope for."

"Maybe so," Elena agreed.

After the young man left, a small boy stepped up to see Elena. He stared at her with huge, round eyes.

"Did you lose something?" she asked him kindly.

The boy nodded but was too tongue-tied to speak.

"Can you tell me what it was?" Elena prompted.

The boy nodded again. Then he opened his mouth wide and pointed to an empty space between his teeth.

"I think I understand," said Elena. "You

lost your two front teeth, right?"

"Yeth," lisped the boy. "Pleath give them back."

Elena shook her head. "I'm sorry. I didn't find any teeth."

The boy looked puzzled. He pointed to her crown. "Aren't you the toof fairy? Mommy thez the toof fairy ith a prinzeth."

"That may be true," said Elena, hiding a smile. "But I'm afraid I'm not her."

"Oh," said the boy sadly.

"Cheer up," Elena called as he turned to leave. "You'll grow new teeth pretty soon!"

It was early evening before Elena had spoken with everyone in line. Most people had lost simple things, like knives and hair ribbons, but one young woman claimed to have lost a glass slipper. "I've read that story, too," Elena said gently.

Not one person mentioned losing a comb, and none of the women who came to the castle had green hair—though one had a streak of bright blue hair and a ring through her nose.

Standing in front of her mirror that night, Elena admired her soft, flowing hair. She couldn't help feeling relieved that no one had come forward to claim the comb. Perhaps the maiden with green hair didn't exist, Elena thought. Maybe her dream was only the result of a guilty conscience—or the rich custard with cream she'd eaten before bedtime.

After placing the comb on her dresser, she snuggled under her bedcovers to read her favorite book of poetry.

As her candle began to burn low, Elena yawned. She hadn't realized how late it was. Setting down her book, she blew out the flame. When she fell asleep, Elena dreamed of the maiden again. Only this time the young woman appeared ill. Her face was ghostly white, and there were dark circles under her eyes. Her beautiful emerald hair looked limp. "Won't you give me back my comb?" the maiden pleaded, just as before. Tears trickled down her pale cheeks. "I'll die if I don't get my comb back. Without it, I can't get home."

★ ★ ★

King Philip ate breakfast with Elena again the next morning. Between bites of scrambled egg and a poppy seed popover, Elena told him all about the green-haired maiden of her dreams—and how no one had come forth to claim the beautiful comb. "Do you think the maiden is real?" Elena asked him. "And if so,

how can I find her?"

King Philip set down his fork. "I believe most dreams show us things we've been thinking of or worrying about. You've always been sensitive, and you've got a keen imagination, so . . ."

"So you don't think she's real?" asked Elena.

Her father nodded. "If you like the comb, I don't see why you shouldn't keep it. After all, you *tried* to find the person who lost it."

"But maybe she doesn't live in our kingdom," said Elena. "Maybe she lives far away."

King Philip's brow furrowed. "I worry about you spending so much time alone," he said after a while. "If only your mother had lived—"

"I'm okay on my own." Elena frowned. Did her father think she'd invented the greenhaired maiden for a companion? It was true she'd been feeling lonelier than usual lately, but she didn't think that had affected her dreams.

"I wish I wasn't always so busy," King Philip continued. "I wonder if you'd like to invite your friends to visit for a few days. It would be good for you to have company."

"Really?" Elena's eyes brightened. "That would be terrific!" Suddenly it didn't matter if her father thought she'd been imagining things. She would get to see her friends! And maybe, just maybe, *they'd* be able to help her solve the mystery of the green-haired maiden.

Princess Preparations

As soon as breakfast was over, King Philip left to attend to royal business. Elena ran down the hall to the castle's Crystal Ball Room. The crystal ball sat on a beautiful ebony table. Elena slid into a chair and stared into the ball. When she asked it to, the ball showed her the Crystal Ball Rooms in all three of her friends' homes.

At first the rooms looked empty. All Elena

could see were vases of flowers and crackling flames in the fireplaces that decorated Crystal Ball Rooms everywhere. But then she saw a flash of movement in her friend Tansy's castle. The ball zoomed in on a freckled face.

Elena felt herself blush. It was Jonah, one of Tansy's six brothers—and, in Elena's opinion, the cutest.

"Hi, Jonah," Elena said. "Is Tansy up?"

A lopsided grin spread across Jonah's face. "Depends on what you mean. If you're talking about where she's at, she's definitely 'up.' But whether she's awake or not, I couldn't say."

Elena laughed. Tansy's bedroom was at the top of a very tall tower.

"Want me to go knock on her door?" Jonah asked.

"Thanks for offering. Would you mind?"

"Not at all. Might take me a little while,

though."

Elena knew the stone steps that wound to Tansy's room were quite a climb. "I'll wait," she said. "Thank you."

Jonah vanished from the ball. As Elena waited for Tansy to appear, she checked on the other two Crystal Ball Rooms again. Lysandra's face floated into view, framed by her beautiful blond waves.

"Hi," Lysandra said. "I was just going to look in on my sister and brother-in-law. What are you up to?"

"I'm waiting for Jonah to fetch Tansy, but I wanted to talk to you and Fatima, too. My father says I can invite you all to visit for a few days."

"Fantastic!" said Lysandra. "I'd love to come!"

The girls chatted till Tansy appeared. Then

Elena repeated her invitation. "You're a life-saver," Tansy said. "I really need to get away for a while. Cole and Ethan are driving me crazy. Last night they mixed hot pepper in my milk. I took a big gulp, and it set my throat on fire."

"That's horrible!" exclaimed Lysandra.

"Poor you," Elena said sympathetically. Cole and Ethan were Tansy's youngest brothers. They had tried to scare the princesses during their last visit—and their plan had worked, too.

The three princesses chatted awhile longer. "If Fatima's able to come, I bet she'll take us to your place," Lysandra said. Fatima had a flying carpet, and the princesses often traveled on it together.

"She's got to come!" said Tansy. "We wouldn't have as much fun without her."

Elena knew what she meant. They all

looked up to Fatima. Not just because she was the oldest of the four girls and had a flying carpet, but because she was so bold. "I'll leave her a message," Elena said. "If all goes well, I'll see you in a few days."

"My fingers are crossed," said Tansy.

"Same here," said Lysandra.

The princesses all said their good-byes. Before leaving the room, Elena scribbled a note inviting Fatima to visit. She propped her note next to the crystal ball, where Fatima would be sure to see it whenever she looked for messages.

On her way back to her room, Elena passed through the Great Hall. She paused to study her mother's portrait, which hung above the fireplace. Elena was surprised to see how much more strongly she resembled her mother now that the comb had tamed her frizzy hair. She wondered if they were alike in other ways, too. Not for the first time, Elena wished she could remember her mother better.

When Elena checked the Crystal Ball Room later that day, she found a note from Fatima waiting for her. She leaned close to the ball to read it. The note said:

> *Hi, Elena,*
> *You bet I'll come! I'll pick up Lysandra*
> *and Tansy along the way. We should arrive*
> *Thursday before lunch. See you soon!*
> > *Lots of love,*
> > *Fatima*

Elena beamed. Her friends would be arriving in just two days!

Not wanting to bother her too-busy father,

Elena took care of all the arrangements for her friends' visit herself. She went over the menus with the Royal Chef, choosing dishes she thought the other princesses would enjoy.

Elena also ordered extra beds for her room so her friends could sleep there too. The Royal Housekeeper let her select the linens. Elena chose lavender satin sheets, then helped the Royal Maid make up each bed.

For the next two nights Elena slept soundly, with no more dreams about the green-haired maiden. It seemed her father must be right: the maiden wasn't real.

Before breakfast on Thursday morning, Elena climbed down to the beach to collect seashells and driftwood. She used them to make a pretty table arrangement.

"That looks nice," King Philip commented as he sat down to eat with her. It was the first meal they'd had together in two days.

"I want everything to be perfect for my friends' visit," Elena said. "I want them to like it here."

"I'm sure they will," said her father. Smiling, he pointed to her table arrangement. "Your mother was good at this kind of thing too. The castle was filled with guests when she was alive. She loved having visitors and worked hard to make everything go smoothly while they were here."

Elena wished they had guests more often, but she knew why they didn't. Her father was always so busy. Yet *she* could help; she'd enjoyed making the arrangements for her friends' visit. At any rate, it pleased her to know she and her mother had more in common than their looks. "Tell me more about my mother," Elena said.

"What do you want to know?" King Philip asked.

"Well, what was she like?"

King Philip stared up at the chandelier, as if the answer could be found there. "She was beautiful," he said at last, "and kind. Your mother liked people, and people liked her."

She must not have been shy then, thought Elena. "Did Mother like poetry?"

"Yes, I think she may have. I know she spent a lot of time reading, anyway."

"I love to read too," said Elena.

"I know you do," said her father.

"Was my mother brave?" Elena asked.

"Oh, very," King Philip answered. "She was probably the bravest person I've ever known. Why, once in the middle of a horrible

thunderstorm, she climbed a tree to rescue a cat that was stuck at the top. The branches were thrashing back and forth in the wind, but that didn't stop her."

"Did she love cats a lot?"

King Philip smiled. "She did. But she loved

you more. That cat was your pet, and you were so frightened when you found her in the tree that your mother was determined to rescue her for you. I only learned later what she had done, or I would have stopped her. It was a very dangerous thing to do."

Elena felt warm all over, having this proof of her mother's love. If only *she* were as brave!

Together Again

AFTER BREAKFAST ELENA CHECKED TO MAKE sure everything was ready for her guests. She went over the menus with the Royal Chef one more time and asked the Royal Maid to bring extra robes and slippers to her room in case any of her friends forgot to pack them. Then she smoothed the sheets on the beds yet again.

Too excited to sit down and read, Elena looked around her room for something else to do. Spying the rainbow-colored comb on top of her dresser, she picked it up. With long, flowing strokes, tangles gave way and her hair became soft and loose. Elena wondered what her mother would think if she could see her now. Would she like how Elena looked? And, more importantly, would her mother be proud of the person she'd become?

Elena was watching from her window when she spotted Fatima's flying carpet in the sky. At first it was only a tiny dot over the sea, but gradually it grew larger, till Elena was able to make out the three princesses seated on top. She ran outside and waved to her friends. They waved excitedly back.

The carpet swooped toward the castle, but it was going too fast. "Whoa!" shouted Fatima, trying to slow it down. It jerked to a halt only inches from Elena and sent all three princesses tumbling over the sides.

"Bats and bullfrogs," muttered Fatima.

Jumping up, she brushed the dirt from her pantaloons, then grinned sheepishly. "Not my best landing, was it? Everyone okay?"

Lysandra and Tansy scrambled to their feet. "Fine," they replied. But when Elena hugged Tansy, she could see her friend had scraped an elbow in the fall.

"Hold on a second," Elena said. Pulling a small blue bottle from the pocket of her gown, she poured out a few drops of creamy lotion. Then she rubbed the lotion over Tansy's elbow. The scrape healed instantly.

"Thanks!" said Tansy.

Elena smiled. "You're welcome." Her magical healing lotion might not be as exciting as Fatima's flying carpet, but it certainly came in handy at times.

Lysandra cocked her head. "You look different, Elena. Did you do something new with your hair?"

"Just combed it, that's all." Elena couldn't

wait to show her friends the rainbow-colored treasure.

Fatima rolled up her carpet and strapped it onto her back. "It must be fun to live on an island," she said.

"It is," said Elena. "I like it a lot."

Lysandra peered down the hill to the sea. "And what a great view!"

"The castle's nice too," said Tansy, squinting up at the red-tiled roof.

Fatima's stomach growled loudly. "Excuse me," she said.

Elena laughed. "You must be hungry after your journey. Let's go inside. Lunch will be waiting for us." She led the princesses into the castle and through the Great Hall.

"Is that your mother?" Lysandra asked, pointing to the portrait over the fireplace.

"Yes," said Elena. "I was three when she died."

"She's very pretty," said Fatima.

Tansy looked from the portrait to Elena and back again. "You look like her," she said.

Elena blushed. "Thank you."

The princesses continued to the Dining Hall, where King Philip was supposed to join them for lunch. But as they sat down to eat, a servant delivered a note on a silver tray. Elena opened the note. Her heart fell as she silently read it:

> *My dearest Elena,*
> *I'm afraid my royal duties will keep me from welcoming your guests at lunch today. I'm so sorry. Please give them my apologies. I promise to see you all at dinner. Have a good time.*
> *Your loving father,*
> *King Philip*

Elena looked up from the note, her eyes meeting Tansy's.

"Is something the matter?" Tansy asked.

To hide her disappointment, Elena smiled. "My father sends his apologies. He's too busy to meet us for lunch, but he'll see us at dinner."

"*Parents,*" Fatima said with sympathy. "They're always busy with something."

"I'm sure it must be something important," Tansy added quickly.

Elena sighed. "It's *all* important. I just wish he didn't have to work so hard."

"Well, we'll see him for dinner, anyway," Lysandra said brightly.

The girls dug into their lunch, which consisted of crabmeat and cucumber sandwiches (without the crusts), apple slices, and blackberry pie.

"That was delicious," Tansy declared when she'd eaten the last bite. "Would it be bad manners if I licked my plate clean?"

"Not if we all do it," said Lysandra, swiping her plate with her tongue.

The princesses laughed.

Fatima pushed back her chair. "I'm stuffed," she said, patting her belly. "Those sandwiches were great."

"I'll tell the chef you liked them," said Elena. She was pleased that her friends had enjoyed the meal she'd chosen.

After lunch Elena showed the princesses to her room.

"Wow, you mean we each get our *own* bed?" asked Tansy. All four girls had shared Tansy's bed when they'd visited her last month. Fortunately, her bed was very wide.

"I want this one!" yelled Fatima, plopping onto the bed closest to the window. Tansy and Lysandra claimed their beds, too.

"I want to show you something," said Elena. She picked up the rainbow-colored comb from her dresser and held it high so that it caught the light pouring in through the window. Her friends oohed and ahhed as the comb shimmered.

Fatima whistled. "That's one gorgeous comb!"

"It sure is," Lysandra said. "Can I hold it?"

Hesitating for just a second, Elena passed it to her. It was hard to let go of the beautiful comb.

"Where did you get it?" asked Tansy as she and Fatima crowded in for a closer look.

Elena told them about discovering the comb on the beach and how she'd tried to find the owner but no one had come to claim it. She didn't mention the green-haired maiden in her dreams, who Elena had decided wasn't real after all.

"Mind if I try it out?" Without waiting for a reply, Lysandra slid the comb through her blond waves. "Fantastic!" she exclaimed. "It doesn't even tug."

Pangs of jealousy stabbed at Elena's heart. The comb was *hers*, not Lysandra's. Lysandra didn't need it. She already had beautiful hair.

"Give it back!" Elena yelled.

Her friends stared at her, looking bewildered. Quickly Lysandra handed her the

comb. "Sorry," she mumbled.

Elena felt terrible. Why had she been so rude? It wasn't like her at all. "Please forgive me," she said. "I don't know what came over me. Of course you may use it."

She was relieved when Lysandra accepted her apology and even asked Elena to comb her hair. Afterward Elena wondered about her strong feelings for the beautiful treasure. Was it possible the comb possessed some kind of magic?

The Dream Returns

Just as he'd promised, King Philip joined the princesses for dinner that night. "What a pleasure to meet you," he said when Elena introduced her friends. "I hope you'll have a wonderful visit here with us."

Everyone seemed to enjoy the food Elena had chosen. The Royal Chef had prepared it perfectly. The roast beef was tender and juicy. The creamed potatoes were rich and smooth.

And the chocolate mousse was delectable.

As they ate, King Philip entertained Elena's friends with tales from his youth. Elena had already heard the story about the time he was chased by a bull while showing off for some princesses, but it still made her laugh.

After dinner the princesses left the castle for a moonlit walk on the beach. As they strolled, the wind rippled through their clothes and tossed their hair. Fatima inhaled. "I just love the smell of the ocean," she said.

Tansy stooped to pick up a shell. "And I could listen to the sound of crashing waves forever."

"Do you remember the spot where you found the comb?" Lysandra asked.

Elena pointed ahead. "It was just past that driftwood log, I think. But closer to the sea." There were no signs of the comb, of course.

Even if it had left marks in the sand, the tides would have swept them away.

By bedtime the princesses were laughing and joking together as if they'd never been apart. As they were getting ready for bed, Elena untangled everyone's windblown hair with her beautiful comb.

"Amazing," said Fatima, running her fingers through her long, dark hair. "It feels so smooth and silky."

Looking in the mirror, Lysandra smiled

and admired her blond waves. "Mine seems softer," she said.

Tansy sat on her bed, polishing her wooden flute with a rag. She patted her short ginger hair. "Mine seems softer too." She blew a few notes on her flute. Like Fatima's flying carpet and Elena's lotion, the flute was magical. When Tansy played it, everyone's thoughts became as clear as if spoken aloud. Tansy always took her flute with her. In fact, Elena couldn't remember

ever seeing her without it.

Lysandra fingered the strap of her purse that never went empty of coins. "If we could find out where the comb came from, I could buy one for each of us," she said.

"That'd be great, wouldn't it?" said Fatima, glancing at Elena.

Elena nodded. But in truth, she liked the idea that the comb was one of a kind.

The princesses talked late into the night until finally, one by one, they drifted off to sleep. Again Elena dreamed about the maiden with the flowing green hair. The young woman's face was thinner than Elena had remembered. Her skin was as pale as moonlight, and her eyes were red rimmed from crying. "Please," begged the maiden in a shaky voice. "I'm dying. Won't you give me back my . . ." But the next word was swallowed up in darkness as the maiden's face faded away.

"NO!" cried Elena. "Don't die! I'll give it back!"

Her shouts woke the others. Fatima lit a candle and hurried to Elena's side. She shook her friend gently. "Wake up."

Slowly, her heart pounding, Elena opened her eyes.

Tansy sat up in bed and yawned. "What's the matter, Elena? Were you having a nightmare?"

Elena took several deep breaths to steady herself. "It was a dream," she explained. "It was one I've had before."

Throwing off her bedcovers, Lysandra sat on the edge of her bed. She looked at Elena curiously. "Please tell us about it."

As Elena described the mysterious green-haired maiden who mourned for her comb, Lysandra's eyes widened. "I was just dreaming

about her too!" she blurted.

"You're kidding, right?" asked Fatima.

Lysandra frowned. "I know it sounds
strange, but it's true."

Pushing herself up onto one elbow, Elena
stared at Lysandra. "If we *both* dreamed
about her, do you think that means she's
real?"

"I have a strong feeling that she is,"

Lysandra said solemnly. "And we've got to find her. We've got to give her back her comb . . . before it's too late!"

Elena shivered. She didn't say what she was thinking—that it might *already* be too late.

The Search

"Do you think the maiden could live somewhere nearby?" asked Fatima.

Elena shook her head. "I don't think so. If she lived nearby, wouldn't she have seen one of my signs and come to claim her comb? Besides, I've never seen anyone around here with green hair."

"But if she's ill, she might be confined to her bed," Lysandra pointed out. "Then she wouldn't know about your signs, and you would never have seen her."

"So what should we do?" asked Tansy. "Knock on every door in the kingdom and ask if anyone knows a girl with green hair?"

"That might work," said Fatima thoughtfully. "But it would also take a long time. And I have a feeling Elena's right about the maiden living far away. So why don't we fly over the island? Let's see if we can spot any houses far from the castle. Those might be the best places to start."

"Good idea," said Elena.

Tansy and Lysandra nodded in agreement.

Fatima opened the bedroom window and leaned out. By now it was almost morning; the sky was growing light. "We should be able to see well in about an hour," she said.

"Just enough time to dress and eat," said Elena.

The princesses changed into their clothes, then went to the Dining Hall for breakfast. Soon a servant appeared with a basket of fresh muffins and pastries, a bowl of boiled eggs, and a tray of cut-up fruit.

As Elena had expected, her father was already at work. She could hear loud, angry voices coming from the Great Hall, where he often met with people. One fisherman was accusing another of purposefully slashing his nets. Elena wondered why anyone would do that, unless they wanted to keep all the fish for themselves. It seemed like such a selfish thing to do. But then Elena remembered how much she'd wanted to keep the maiden's comb for herself. She hoped her father was able to sort everything out so the fishermen could be friends.

Back in her room after breakfast, Elena tucked the beautiful rainbow-colored comb into her pocket. She'd be sad to part with it, but she couldn't let the green-haired maiden die!

Soon the princesses were ready to go. Fatima unrolled her flying carpet, and the girls seated themselves on top. "Hang on tight!" Fatima exclaimed. She pulled up the front edge of the carpet, and they sailed through Elena's open window.

They flew to the center of the island first, then spiraled outward to search for houses hidden among the trees. Whenever they spotted one, Fatima would land the carpet nearby, and two princesses would hop off to see if anyone living there had green hair.

After a dozen or more unsuccessful searches, the girls were beginning to lose hope of ever finding the green-haired maiden. Then Lysandra spotted a small cottage hidden in a clump of trees. Fatima landed the carpet, and Elena and Lysandra jumped off to investigate.

When they knocked on the cottage door, a boy about their age answered. Dressed in a ragged shirt and faded leggings, he was very thin, and his face could have used a good scrubbing. "Hello," he said, staring at them. "Who are you?"

Elena was used to the staring by now. These people probably didn't get many visitors. She politely introduced herself and Lysandra.

The boy scratched his head. "I didn't know old King Philip had a daughter," he said. "Fancy you showing up here! No one usually bothers with us. Me and my sister, we've been living here all alone since before I can remember. Our parents died when I was just a baby."

Elena wasn't sure she liked this boy calling her father "old," and it had been rather embarrassing to find out just how many people didn't know she existed. But she promised herself that whatever happened in their search for the maiden, she'd make sure she brought these people to her father's attention. Most of them were so very poor. Surely there was *something* her father could do to make their lives a little easier.

"We're looking for a maiden with green hair," said Lysandra.

"Oh, you mean my sister," the boy said matter-of-factly.

Elena's heart beat fast. "Where is she? Will you introduce us to her?"

The boy shrugged. "Sure," he said. "But I don't know why you'd want to meet her. I'd keep away from her if I were you. She's always teasing."

Elena and Lysandra followed him into the cottage. It was dark inside and reeked of onions and garlic. "Wanda!" bellowed the boy. "There're two girls here to see you! They say they're *princesses*."

"Sure they are, Eric!" a voice yelled back. "And I'm Rumpelstiltskin. Tell them to come back tomorrow. I'm too busy spinning straw

into gold right now."

From around the corner came a large girl wearing a wide brown skirt and a dirty white blouse. Elena's face fell when she saw that the girl's hair—which hung in two long braids—was not green at all, but a bright shade of red.

The girl's jaw dropped when she saw Elena and Lysandra standing inside the

cottage. Both princesses had dressed in simple gowns, but, even so, their dresses must've seemed awfully grand to this young woman. Her braids fell forward as she curtsied clumsily. "Your Majesties," she said in awe.

"Please," said Elena. "That's not necessary. We're sorry to have troubled you. You see, we're looking for a maiden with green hair, and your brother said—"

"Shh," said Wanda, holding a finger to her lips. She took the princesses aside. "About my brother . . . he doesn't see colors so well. Least not red and green. They both look the same to him. So, just to have a little fun, I told him my hair was green." She looked at them anxiously. "No harm in that, is there? Being there's just the two of us? You won't tell him the truth, will you?"

Lysandra grinned. "It's a fine joke."

Elena nodded in agreement. "We won't give you away," she whispered. "But I guess you don't know anyone who *really* has green hair?"

"No," Wanda replied. "Like I said, there's only the two of us around here."

After saying good-bye, Elena and Fatima rejoined their friends on the carpet. As they sailed over the cottage, they could see Wanda and Eric watching them. All four princesses waved. The boy pointed at Tansy excitedly. "Look, Wanda!" they heard him yell. "That girl's got green hair too!"

Elena and Lysandra laughed. While Lysandra explained the joke to the others, Elena decided that she would send Wanda and Eric some new clothes after she got back to the castle. It was one thing she could do to help, anyway.

"Where to now?" asked Fatima.

"I don't know," Elena admitted. She was afraid that time was running out. What if their search for the green-haired maiden ended in failure?

Seals

THE PRINCESSES FLEW TWO MORE LOOPS AROUND the island, stopping at eight homes, but found no trace of the green-haired maiden. "Shall we keep going?" asked Fatima.

"Let's fly along the beach one more time," Elena suggested. Starting over the castle, they flew past fishing villages and a bay, then circled toward the opposite side of the island.

Hours ago, when they'd first begun their search, the ocean had been a beautiful blue-green color. But now it was a greenish gray, and the waves were choppy. Clouds had moved in, covering the sun, and a strong wind blew, making it harder for Fatima to control her carpet. "Sorry about the bumpy ride," she said as the carpet bucked up and down.

Elena grasped the edges and held on tight, hoping the storm would hold off till they were back at the castle.

"I see something!" Tansy said suddenly.

Everyone looked down. Elena drew in her breath. At first glance it looked like a body was lying on the beach—a still body with long green hair. But as Fatima flew closer, the princesses saw that the "body" was just a driftwood log and the hair a clump of seaweed. The girls laughed with relief.

As they flew on, Elena spotted a colony of seals on some rocks out to sea. She pointed toward them, and Fatima zoomed in for a closer look. Among the grown-up seals were several young pups. They seemed to be having a lot of fun, in spite of the choppy water. They slid off the rocks into the sea, bobbed up and down, and slapped the surface with their front flippers. *Maa, maa*, they cried, sounding almost like sheep.

"They're so cute!" cried Lysandra. "I wish I knew Seal so I could talk to them."

Tansy pulled her flute from her pocket. "Even if we don't know what they're saying, at least we can find out what they're *thinking*."

Fatima cocked her head. "Your flute works on *animals*?"

"Yup," said Tansy. "I've tried it on dogs before. Their thoughts aren't very interesting, though. All they think about is food."

Elena suspected that was what seals thought about, too. And she was right. When Tansy began to play her flute, the thoughts that floated up from below were all about fish.

Boy, I'd really love to catch a fish right now, thought one seal. *I'm so hungry I could eat a whale!*

That last fish I ate was scrumptious, thought a second seal. *I could eat a zillion more like it.*

The princesses' ears *really* perked up, how-

ever, when they heard the thoughts of a third seal: *I saw a funny-looking fish in a cave this morning. It cried because it lost something and wanted to go home.*

Tansy nearly dropped her flute in surprise! The girls all looked at one another. "Do you suppose it's *her*?" asked Lysandra.

"In my dreams the maiden was always surrounded by darkness," said Elena.

"Like in a *cave*?" asked Tansy.

Elena nodded. "Exactly."

"How many caves are on this island?" Fatima asked.

"Just one." Elena frowned. "It's called the Cave of No Hope."

"Sounds like a nice place," joked Fatima.

"There are rumors that sea monsters live inside that cave," Elena said with a shudder. "Fishermen say those who enter never come out."

Fatima tossed her long black hair. "Nonsense! People say all sorts of things, but that doesn't mean they're true."

"That's for sure," agreed Tansy.

Elena wondered if she was thinking about their last adventure together, and all the rumors the villagers had spread about the ogre in Tansy's kingdom.

"I say we go into this cave and search for the maiden," said Lysandra.

The three princesses looked at Elena.

Trying to keep her voice from shaking, she murmured, "Okay." She wished she felt as brave as the others—and as brave as her mother had been.

"All right!" said Lysandra. "It'll be an adventure."

Tansy leaned forward on the carpet. "Let's go!"

"Not yet," said Fatima. "Don't you think we should make a few preparations? After all, we're not like those silly princes who go galloping after fire-breathing dragons without a plan, right? Wouldn't you think they'd take a few blankets to smother the flames, or even a jug of water?"

The others laughed. "Well, the ocean will flood the cave when the tide comes in," said Elena. "But with a flying carpet, that shouldn't be a problem. Still, when you're around water, it never hurts to carry a rope. And we'll need a lantern, since the cave will be dark."

"How about some apples?" suggested Lysandra.

Fatima raised an eyebrow. "Apples?"

Lysandra shrugged. "I'm hungry. Besides, if there really are sea monsters, we'll have something to feed them so they won't eat *us*."

"I'm not sure sea monsters would be content with only fruit," Fatima said.

"There's a shop in a fishing village not far from here," said Elena. "They should have everything we need."

So off they flew to the shop. With coins from her magical purse, Lysandra bought a coil of rope, a lantern, and a bag of ripe, red apples. Then the four princesses climbed back onto the carpet and took off for the Cave of No Hope, with Elena showing the way.

"Delicious," said Lysandra, munching on one of the apples.

As the girls neared the cave, the wind

picked up again. It sent waves crashing against the rocks and spraying high into the air. From within the cave came a loud, fierce roaring. "Whoa," said Fatima, bringing the carpet to a halt. "Whatever's inside there sounds pretty angry."

Elena clasped her hands together to keep them from trembling.

"Maybe those rumors weren't rumors after all," said Tansy. Her eyes looked huge.

"D-do you think we should turn back?" Lysandra stuttered.

Why, they're just as scared as I am, thought Elena. "Why don't you play your flute, Tansy?" she suggested. "If there *are* any sea monsters inside, maybe we can hear what they're thinking."

"Good idea," said the others.

Tansy pulled out her flute and began to play, but no thoughts floated out of the cave.

"Maybe it doesn't work on sea monsters," said Lysandra.

"Shh," said Fatima, putting a finger to her lips. "I think I hear something."

The four girls listened carefully. Finally, above the roaring, they heard a faint cry: "Where is my comb? I want to go home."

The princesses stared at one another. Elena took a deep breath. "We have to go inside."

Into the Cave

ELENA TRIED TO LIGHT THE LANTERN, BUT THE wind kept blowing out the flame. Finally the wick caught, and the lantern began to glow. The princesses held their breaths as Fatima flew the carpet into the mouth of the cave. A huge wave pounded against the sides when they entered. Cold salt water sprayed down on them, making them scream.

The light cast eerie shadows against the

walls, but as the girls flew deeper into the cave, the roaring grew quiet. It had only been the *wind* making those sounds, Elena realized with relief. No wonder Tansy's flute hadn't been able to pick up the thoughts of any sea monsters. There *weren't* any sea monsters. Not in here, at least.

Suddenly something small and dark swooped toward them. It was a bat! Startled, Fatima threw her hands up to cover her face. The carpet jerked, and she tumbled off. There was a splash as she hit the water below.

"Help!" she cried. "I can't swim!"

The other three princesses grabbed the sides of the carpet so they wouldn't be thrown off too. "Lie on your back and kick your feet!" Elena shouted to Fatima as the carpet came to a halt. She passed the lantern to Lysandra, then grabbed the coil of rope. Holding tightly to one end, she cast the rest toward Fatima. "Hold on!" she yelled.

Fatima thrashed around until she found the rope. Then Lysandra and Tansy held on to Elena as she towed Fatima to a rock that jutted out of the water. Gasping for breath, Fatima scrambled to the top. With halting jerks and bumps, Lysandra guided the carpet close enough for Fatima to climb aboard.

"Th-th-that was close," Fatima said through chattering teeth. She was drenched.

"Here." Elena removed her cloak and wrapped it around her friend. "It won't help much, but it'll keep you a little warmer till we get back to the castle."

"Th-thanks," said Fatima.

As the girls sped forward with Fatima at the helm once again, the river below narrowed to a thin stream. They could hear the maiden crying now. Her sobs sounded faint at first but grew louder as the princesses flew deeper into the cave. Rounding a bend, they finally came upon the maiden, lying in the shallow water. Her emerald hair, which flowed to her waist, shimmered in the lantern's light. The carpet swooped toward her and she cried out in alarm. As the maiden began thrashing about, like she was trying to get away, the princesses caught a glimpse of her blue-and-green-scaled tail.

"She's a mermaid!" Elena exclaimed.

Fatima landed the carpet on a rock beside the stream, and the princesses climbed off.

"Don't be afraid," said Elena as they approached the mermaid. "We're here to help you."

The mermaid stopped whipping her tail around. She lay on her side, breathing rapidly. Her face was even paler than Elena remembered from her dreams. Then the mermaid shifted her tail, and Elena saw a big gash in it.

"You've been hurt!" she cried.

The mermaid groaned. "I was caught in a fishing net at the bottom of the sea and dragged over some sharp rocks."

"How awful!" Lysandra exclaimed.

The others nodded in agreement. "I may be able to heal your tail if you'll let me try," Elena offered.

The mermaid stiffened. "How?"

Elena pulled out her small blue bottle. "A few drops of this lotion should do the trick," she said, hoping it would work as well on mermaids as it did on humans.

"Will it sting?" the mermaid asked anxiously.

"Not at all," Elena assured her. Opening the bottle, she poured out a few drops of the magical lotion, then carefully rubbed it over the mermaid's wound. The mermaid winced a little when Elena touched her, but as the gash healed over, the look of pain left her face. She swished her tail from side to side to test it out. "Thank you," she said graciously. "It's as good as new!"

"You're welcome," said Elena. She told the mermaid her name and introduced her friends. "We're princesses, but we're all from different kingdoms."

"My name is Sophie," said the mermaid. "And I'm a princess too."

"How did you escape from the net?" Tansy asked.

"I used a broken clam shell to saw through it, but then I washed up in this cave. I might have been able to swim out if I hadn't hurt my tail, but I was too weak." She paused. "I don't know what would've happened to me if you hadn't come. . . ." Her voice trailed off.

"Well, you should be fine now," said Fatima. "If you'd like, we can fly you out of the cave on my carpet."

"I'd love to fly with you," said Sophie, "but I need to stay in the water. Only it's so shallow here that it will be hard for me to swim."

"I know!" said Elena. "We can *tow* you out!" She showed Sophie the rope. "If you hold on to one end while we fly, we can pull you to the mouth of the cave."

"Thank you," said Sophie. Yet she still seemed troubled. "The problem is, even if I do get out, I won't be able to find my way home." A tear trickled down her cheek. "The mermaid kingdom is hidden to protect us from the outside world. Beyond its gates, it's invisible."

Tansy scratched her head. "Then how did you get caught in a fishing net?"

Sophie blushed. "Sometimes I sneak out through the gates to explore other parts of the sea."

"But how did you find your way back those other times?" asked Lysandra.

"My grandmother gave me a special comb. No matter how far away I wander, it always points the way back." Sophie hung her head. "But I lost it when I was struggling to get out of the net."

Reaching into her pocket, Elena pulled out the rainbow-colored comb. She *knew* there was something magical about it. "Is this it?" she asked.

Back to Sea

SOPHIE'S EYES LIT UP. "HOW DID YOU FIND IT?"

Elena explained how she'd been walking along the beach when the comb washed ashore. With a pang of regret, she handed the beautiful treasure to Sophie. The mermaid was so delighted to have it back, she flicked her tail up and down, making little splashes in the shallow stream.

"I saw your face in my dreams," Elena said,

"and I heard you crying. Still, I wasn't sure you were real."

"But then I dreamed about you too," said Lysandra.

"So we tried to find you," continued Fatima. "Only we didn't know you were a mermaid, so we checked on land first."

Then Tansy chimed in. She told about playing her flute above the seals, and how the thoughts of one seal gave them the clue that led to the cave.

Hugging her comb, Sophie exclaimed, "I'm so lucky you found me!"

"When we reached the cave, we almost turned back," Tansy admitted. "We heard roaring and thought there were sea monsters."

"But Elena convinced us to go on," Lysandra said.

"And she rescued me when I fell into the water and couldn't swim," added Fatima.

Sophie smiled at Elena. "You must be very brave," she said.

"I was probably more afraid than anyone," Elena confessed.

Sophie flicked her tail. "My grandmother always says, 'Only fools are never afraid.' She told me that true courage is facing your fears and going forward."

"Your grandmother sounds very wise," said Fatima.

Elena wondered if her mother had been afraid when she'd rescued that cat during the storm. Perhaps she had. And maybe Elena was more like her mother than she'd thought, in spite of her frizzy brown hair. It made her feel good to think so.

"Your family must be so worried," said Lysandra. "Do you suppose they've been searching for you?"

Sophie nodded. "They'll have emptied out

the nets of every passing boat and searched the entire ocean floor by now. But I'm sure no one knows about this cave. Even if they do, it would be too difficult to reach."

"Maybe we should go," said Elena. "Then your family can stop worrying."

With Sophie holding on to the rope, Elena and her friends towed the mermaid out of the cave. When they reached the sea, Sophie let go. "Thanks!" she called to them as she bobbed up and down in the waves. "I'll be fine now."

Fatima lowered the carpet so that it hovered just above the water's surface. Elena leaned over toward Sophie. "Are you sure you'll be okay?" she asked anxiously. "I wish there was a way for us to know when you've made it home safely."

Sophie thought for a moment. "I know! I'll send you a sign."

"What kind of a sign?" asked Lysandra.

The mermaid smiled. "You'll know. Just look to the sky." Then with a flick of her tail, she dove into the water.

Elena watched the ripples spread, trying to fix in her mind the spot where Sophie had disappeared.

Since they'd left the cave, the wind had died down and the sea had become blue again. Now the clouds parted, and the sun came out. Even so, Fatima shivered.

"You're still damp," said Elena. "We'd better get back to the castle so you can change into dry clothes."

"I'd like to take a long, hot bath as soon as we arrive," Fatima said, pointing the carpet toward shore.

As they approached the castle, Elena turned to gaze back at the sea. "Look!" she cried. Starting from the spot where they'd last seen the mermaid, a brightly colored rainbow stretched across the sky.

"It's Sophie's sign!" exclaimed Lysandra.

Tansy shielded her eyes from the sun. "I can only see one end of the rainbow."

Elena smiled. She was sure she knew where the other end was—in the invisible, hidden kingdom of the mermaids. Sophie was home.

In the Castle

FATIMA LANDED THE CARPET SMOOTHLY, AND the four girls started for the castle. Before they could reach the gates, however, the front doors were flung open and a servant came rushing out.

"Princess Elena!" the servant exclaimed. "Thank goodness you're back! Your father has been asking for you. He was taken ill hours ago. The doctor is with him now."

Elena's heart began to beat fast. "What happened?" she asked as the princesses followed the servant inside the castle.

"I don't know for sure, Your Highness. But here's what I heard: King Philip fainted in the Great Hall this morning. He'd been meeting with two fishermen about some kind of problem. They'd just turned to leave when your father collapsed. They're the ones who let everyone know."

"Oh no!" cried Elena. She turned toward her friends. "I must go see him."

"Of course," said Fatima. "Don't worry about us. We'll go to your room and wait for you there."

Elena raced through the castle to her father's chamber. The Royal Doctor, an elderly man with a full head of white hair, was just coming out. Closing the door behind him, he stopped Elena. "No one can go in just now," he told her. "King Philip needs his rest."

"But I'm his daughter. I *must* see him!" Elena insisted.

The doctor blinked. "Oh, excuse me, Your Highness. But I would still advise you to wait awhile. Your father has been working much too hard. He must have peace and quiet if he is to fully recover."

"Elena?" King Philip called through the door. "Is that you?"

"Yes, Father," Elena called back.

"Come in. I want to see you."

Elena looked at the doctor. He rolled his eyes. "All right," he said, "but try not to overexcite him. And only stay for a few minutes. He really needs to sleep."

"Don't worry," said Elena. "I'll do just as you say."

King Philip was lying in bed, a blanket

drawn up to his chin. Elena hurried over to him. She bent down and kissed the top of his bald head. "I'm sorry you're ill," she said.

"Doctors!" her father grunted in disgust. "They don't know everything."

"Yes, but they do know *some* things," Elena said gently. "I've always thought you worked too hard."

"Really?" For a moment her father looked surprised. Then he sighed. "Well, I suppose you're right. I know it's kept me from spending as much time with you as I'd like." He laid a hand on her arm. "Have I been a bad father?"

"No!" Elena exclaimed. "But why don't you let *me* help with the running of the kingdom? Then you wouldn't have to work so hard."

King Philip stared at the ceiling. "But you

shouldn't have to worry about the kingdom's affairs. You should just read, and go for long walks on the beach, and do whatever else young girls like to do."

"But I have *too* much time to do those things," Elena protested. "I like working. Last

week I made the arrangements for my friends' visit, and it was fun. I even chose the menus all by myself."

Her father nodded. "So you did. And you made good choices, too. The meals this week have been excellent."

Elena beamed. "I could do other things if you'd let me."

"I do believe you could." He raised his head from his pillow. "So tell me what you and your friends have been up to today. You were gone a long time."

Elena couldn't help noticing the circles under her father's eyes, and that he was stifling a yawn.

"May I tell you about our adventure later?" she asked. "It's not a short story, and I promised the doctor I wouldn't stay long. He says you need to rest."

Her father sank back into his pillow. "I suppose he's right," King Philip said tiredly. "But I want to hear all about it later."

Elena kissed her father on the cheek and then tiptoed out of his room, closing the door quietly behind her. As she entered the Great

Hall, she heard voices raised in argument. Two fishermen were hurling insults at each other and landing the occasional punch.

"STOP!" Elena commanded.

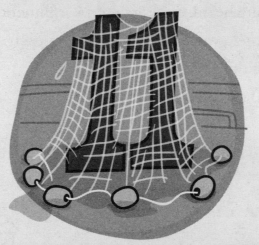

The Feuding Fishermen

THE FISHERMEN BLINKED. ONE WAS TALL AND
thin, and the other was short and squat. "Who
are you?" they asked at the same time.

Elena sighed. "I'm King Philip's daughter,
Princess Elena."

The men bowed awkwardly. "Sorry,
Princess, we didn't recognize you," the tall
fisherman mumbled.

Holding her chin high, Elena sat down in

her father's chair. "My father is ill and needs to rest," she said, "but perhaps I can help if you'll just tell me what you were fighting about."

Both fishermen started to talk at once.

"One at a time, please," said Elena. She pointed to the tall fisherman. "You first."

The tall fisherman stepped foward. "He cut up my nets again, Your Highness. How am I supposed to make a living when all my fish escape?"

"He's lying!" shouted the short fisherman. "But it serves him right—especially after what he did to *my* nets."

"I keep telling you, I didn't touch your nets," growled the tall fisherman.

"Wait a minute," said Elena. "Are you the same two fishermen who spoke with my father this morning—just before he collapsed?"

The two fishermen scowled at each other, then nodded.

"Well, what did my father tell you to do?" asked Elena.

They stared at the floor. "He told us to leave each other's nets alone," mumbled the short fisherman.

"And did you?" Elena asked gently.

"*I* did," declared the tall fisherman, glaring at the short fisherman. "But *he* didn't. When I hauled in my nets this afternoon, they were all cut up again."

The short fisherman glared back. "So were mine!"

"I see," said the tall fisherman. "So you think I just swam underwater and slashed your nets with a knife when you weren't looking?"

The short fisherman crossed his arms over his chest. "Maybe," he said.

An idea was starting to form in Elena's

mind. "When did this net-cutting business first start?" she asked.

The short fisherman frowned. "Four days ago," he said, counting on his fingers. "No, five."

Aha! thought Elena. It was five days ago that she'd found Sophie's comb! And hadn't Sophie said that her family would have emptied the nets of every passing boat to look for her? Now Elena remembered that Sophie had used a broken clam shell to free herself. It must've been Sophie's family who had cut through the fishermen's nets!

She thought about telling the fishermen, but they probably wouldn't believe her. And it would be worse if they did. Who knew what they might do then? Sophie's kingdom was hidden, but the merpeople did occasionally leave its borders. Elena had to protect Sophie

and her family.

"I don't believe either of you cut the other's nets," Elena said finally. "Maybe your nets tore on some sharp rocks."

"But we've always fished in the same spot and never had any trouble with torn nets before," protested the tall fisherman.

"Perhaps," said Elena, "but things change." She hoped they wouldn't question her about this. After all, it wasn't likely that big, heavy rocks would move around on the ocean

floor. "If you move your boats to another spot, I don't believe you'll have any more trouble."

The fishermen just looked at her.

"And . . . and that's an order!" Elena finished.

"Yes, Princess," the fishermen said in unison. Bowing, they left the Great Hall.

Even if they didn't follow her advice, Elena thought, their nets would be safe now that Sophie was home. And King Philip would have one less argument to settle. She couldn't wait to tell him. He would be so surprised to learn about the mermaid, too!

Elena hopped down from her father's chair. As she passed by the fireplace, she glanced up at the portrait of her mother. The look in Queen Helen's eyes and the smile on her face seemed to say, "Well done, my daughter." Filled with joy, Elena raced down the hall to join her friends.

Check out all the Princess Power adventures!

Princess Power #1:
The Perfectly Proper Prince

Princess Lysandra finds sewing, napping, and decorating the palace to be extremely boring. She wants adventure! So when Lysandra meets Fatima, Elena, and Tansy, she couldn't be happier. But their first quest comes even sooner than expected, when they stumble upon a frog that just *might* have royal blood running through his veins.

Princess Power #2:
The Charmingly Clever Cousin

Princess Fatima doesn't care much for her brother-in-law, Ahmed. His cousin Yusuf is much more charming, with ___ tricks. Yet ___ nd never ___ picious is ___ s to come

The Awfully Angry Ogre

Princess Tansy knows that whenever something terrible occurs in her kingdom, the ogre gets the blame. Yet anyone who challenges him is turned to stone! Tansy's two oldest brothers have been forbidden to fight the ogre, but they're determined to try. Can Tansy and her friends save the boys from a horrible fate?

Princess Power #4:
The Mysterious, Mournful Maiden

Princess Elena is excited to find a treasure on the beach—a beautiful comb that tames and softens her frizzy hair. However, she soon starts dreaming of a green-haired maiden who cries that she can't live without her comb. The princesses all want to help. But will they be able to find the maiden . . . before it's too late?

HarperTrophy®
An Imprint of HarperCollinsPublishers

www.harpercollinschildrens.com